For Charlotte and Jake

First U.S. edition 2017

Library of Congress Catalog Card Number pending
ISBN 978-0-7636-8186-9

17 18 19 20 21 22 APS 10 9 8 7 6 5 4 3 2 1

Printed in Humen, Dongguan, China

This book was typeset in Burbank Big Regular.
The illustrations were done in ink and colored digitally.

Candlewick Press
99 Dover Street
Somerville, Massachusetts 02144

visit us at www.candlewick.com

PIGSTICKS AND HAROLD

LOST IN TIME!

Alex Milway

CANDLEWICK PRESS

The Junky Spaceship

USS ENTERPIG

The Tuptown Science Fair started in an hour, and Pigsticks was beginning to worry. He was trying to make a spaceship for the Best Invention competition, but so far all he'd made was a mess.

Harold had told him that everyone else had already prepared their inventions.

PIRATE GEORGE'S DIVING SUIT

For formal underwater occasions.

BOBBINS THE ANGRY MOUSE'S CALMING SALTS

Never be angry again! (Unless something really annoying happens.)

ALICE ANTEATER'S ROBOTIC BUTTERFLY FEEDER

Spoil butterflies from the comfort of your sofa!

SISSY PORCUPINE'S GIANT CARROT

For when you really need to see in the dark!

EVIE BIRD'S INFLATABLE TREE

Ideal for the bird on the go.

OTTERLY'S PORTABLE LIGHTHOUSE

Never leave a dangerous rock unlit.

BONZO'S SUPER-HAMMER

For when you have too many nails and too little time.

BENJAMIN HORSE'S MEGA-LOUD GUITAR

Everyone will listen to your music! (They won't have a choice.)

HAROLD'S BEST-EVER BATTENBURG CAKE

Scientifically proven to be extra pink and delicious.

ADA LOVEPIG

"Unless I get this spaceship right, I'll lose the competition," said Pigsticks. "And I never lose anything! Except my socks. They always go missing."

"Try tweaking the warp drive," said Harold.

"It doesn't have a warp drive," said Pigsticks. "It's powered by batteries."

Harold could see why the spaceship didn't work.

"You know, my great-aunt Ada Lovepig was a brilliant inventor," said Pigsticks with a sigh. "I just need to be more like her."

"Hold on!" said Harold. "What are you sitting on?"

Pigsticks looked at his seat. It was covered in dials and switches, and what he'd thought was an armrest was actually a lever. Carved on the front were the words *LOVEPIG TIME MACHINE*.

WARNING: VERY RUSTY AND FRAGILE!

-65000000

LOVEPIG TIME MACHINE

LOVEPIG
TIME MACHINE

1. **PADDED BOTTOM PROTECTOR** A comfy seat. Fits mammals and reptiles. Not suitable for fish.

2. **INTERDIMENSIONAL TIME COGS** Old-fashioned but effective at keeping the hands of time turning.

3. **HOME-TIME DISPLAY** Never miss a party in the present —— keep one eye on the home-time clock.

4. **YEAR DISPLAY** Shows the exact point in time you're traveling to —— responds to the Quantum Leap Lever.

5. **ON/OFF SWITCH** If the time machine doesn't work, try turning it off and on again.

6. **THE SPACE BRACE** A supportive back rest to keep you upright during time hops.

7. **QUANTUM LEAP LEVER** Pull this to set your desired time period destination.

8. **TRAVEL GAMES** For passing the time as you pass through time.

9. **EMERGENCY OVEN** For time periods without kitchens.

10. **VORTEX BATTERY** Works in any conditions, guaranteed to last long into the future and far into the past.

"A time machine?" cried Harold, stepping back in case he disappeared into the past.

"Great-Aunt Ada must have made it!" said Pigsticks. "This was her workshop! She was a genius. She invented boarband Internet and spam mail, too — but, then, everyone makes mistakes."

Harold looked at the time machine. "Do you think it actually works?" he said. "It's very old. . . ."

"Let's see," said Pigsticks. He pressed a switch, and a bright-yellow light flickered on. He was so excited that his tail curled into a ball.

"Success!" he cried. "The Best Invention Prize will be mine! We can use the time machine to go into the future and learn how to build a real spaceship."

"We?" said Harold.

"There are two seats," said Pigsticks. "Perfect for a time traveler and his assistant!"

"But I'm happy in the present," said Harold. "Anyway, it's a terrible idea. Look how rusty that time lever is."

"We can't let a bit of rust stand in our way!" cried Pigsticks. "If we travel through time, we'll be legends! They'll talk about us forever!"

Harold didn't want to be talked about forever.

"But Harold," said Pigsticks, "think of the cakes!"

"Cakes?" said Harold. He wasn't sure what cakes had to do with time travel, but he was definitely interested all the same.

"Yes!" said Pigsticks. "Imagine all the future cakes that no one's invented yet, and all the ancient cakes that no longer exist!"

Harold imagined the cakes. They were delicious.

"So," said Pigsticks, "are you coming?"

"Hang on," said Harold, grabbing his bag. "We'll need my Best-Ever Battenburg for the journey."

MOLECULE MERINGUE

A fizz-whizzer of a sponge cake, filled with buzzing protons and topped with tongue-popping sugary electrons.

GREAT PYRAMID CAKE

A triple-decker gâteau filled with strawberry jam and cream, topped with a single strawberry for good measure.

CAKEHENGE

A structural treat built with éclairs and topped off with lashings of chocolate.

Harold took his seat on the time machine and held on tight.

"To the future!" cried Pigsticks.

"To the cakes!" cried Harold.

Pigsticks pulled the lever. There was a *clunk* and a *crack*.

"Er — Pigsticks?" said Harold as the world began to blur. "Was the lever meant to break off in your hand?"

Stuck in Time

VWORP!
VWORP!

Traveling through time was a lot like falling down a very large, very scary drain. Pigsticks and Harold spun in circles as history flashed before their eyes. Then, with a *thud,* the machine stopped.

"This doesn't look like the future," whispered Harold. "This looks like . . ."

"The time of the dinopigs!"

"We're in the past," said Pigsticks. "How interesting."

"It's not interesting. It's terrifying!" whispered Harold, edging away from a Tyrannosaurus Pig. "And the time machine is broken! We can't control where we travel to without the lever! How will we ever get home?"

"We need to find something to replace the broken lever," said Pigsticks. "What about that stick?"

He pointed to a branch lying in a pile of dinopig eggs. "You fetch it. I'll guard the time machine."

"If you think so. . . ." said Harold, reaching out.

Harold leaped onto the time machine, empty-handed. "Quick!" he cried. "Let's get out of here!"

Pigsticks gave the machine a thump, and soon they were spinning through time. "Wherever we end up, it'll be better than there," he said as they crash-landed again. But Pigsticks was wrong.

19

"We're in ancient Egypt!" cried Harold.

"What a wonderful view," said Pigsticks as

they slid down a pyramid. "This must

be the reign of . . ."

"Cleopigtra!" said Pigsticks. "And there she is!"

"How dare you use my favorite pyramid as a slide!" cried Cleopigtra, waving a scary-looking staff at them. "It's covered in pure gold!"

"And very tasteful it is, too," said Pigsticks.

"We're very sorry," said Harold. And then he realized: Cleopigtra's staff would be the perfect replacement for the broken time lever. . . .

"Pigsticks," he hissed. "The staff."

"A giraffe?" said Pigsticks, his ears a bit clogged from time traveling.

"No! Cleopigtra's stick," said Harold.

"She feels sick?" said Pigsticks.

"What are you two muttering about?" asked Cleopigtra, her eyes narrowing.

"We were wondering, Your . . . Royalness," said Harold. "Could we please borrow your staff?"

"HOW DARE YOU!" roared Cleopigtra. "Only a pharaoh can touch this staff. It belonged to Pigothep the Third. Guards! Lock them up!"

"Quick, Harold," whispered Pigsticks. "Go on. Let's get out of here!"

Pigsticks and Harold jumped backward and forward through time. They looked everywhere for something to replace the broken time lever, but they had no luck.

There was nothing in London, where they got a nice warm welcome — a bit too warm for Harold's liking.

What's so great about this fire?

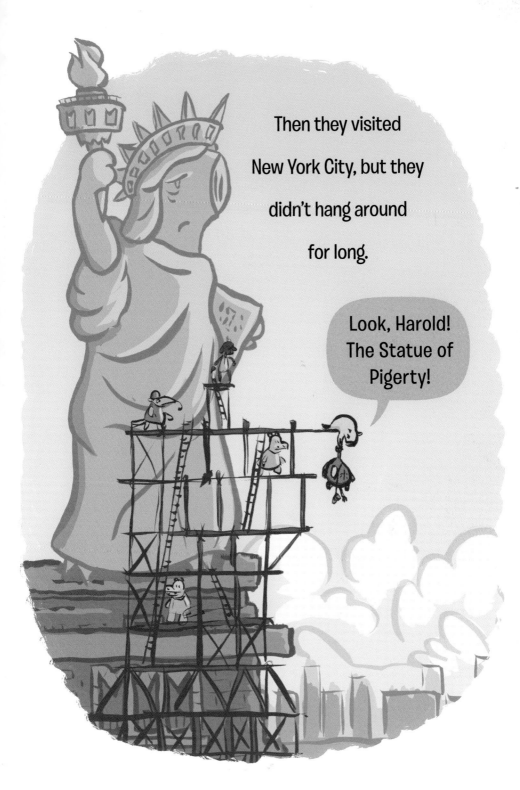

Then they visited
New York City, but they
didn't hang around
for long.

Look, Harold!
The Statue of
Pigerty!

25

They bumped into Julius Squealer and found themselves at the sharp end of the law in ancient Rome.

Harold was starting to feel time-travel-sick.

"Isn't history exciting?" said Pigsticks.

"In books, yes," said Harold. "In real life, it's downright dangerous. And I haven't eaten a single cake yet. I just want to fix our time machine and get back home. . . ."

He screwed his eyes up tight as the time machine landed again — on something soft. . . .

"This place looks rather nice!" said Pigsticks.

"I'm not so sure," said Harold. "I can see some very angry-looking boats. . . ."

"Oh, nonsense," said Pigsticks. "I have a good

feeling this time. The air's clear,

the view is stunning—"

"And the time machine is

sinking!" cried Harold.

CRASH!

They fell through the roof of a smoke-filled building.

A lot of very angry eyes were staring down at them.

"OH, NO!" cried Harold. "VIKINGS!"

The Viking chief stormed up to them, waving her terrifying ax.

"She doesn't look happy," whispered Harold.

"Quite the opposite," whispered Pigsticks.

"I am Hamfrida, chief of the village!" she cried. "You fell from the sky on your silver throne and ruined our midsummer party!"

Harold felt terrible. There was nothing worse than someone ruining your party, especially if you hadn't had cake yet. "We're ever so sorry," he said.

"You will pay for this!" Hamfrida growled.

"But we don't have any money!" said Pigsticks.

"We don't want your money," said Hamfrida. "We will take your freedom! We will burn your silver throne to celebrate midsummer and banish you to the ice lands . . . FOREVER!"

"FOREVER?" said Pigsticks.

"FOREVER!" said Hamfrida.

"Forever is a very long time," said Harold.

"And it starts RIGHT NOW!" said Hamfrida.

"No, it doesn't!" said Pigsticks. He grabbed Harold's hand, and they ran into the Viking village. The streets were littered with stinky dried fish, and the vicious Vikings were everywhere, tossing axes at them and shouting scary words.

Soon they were trapped in a dead end.

"Pigsticks," said Harold, "this is the end

of the road. It's been nice knowing you...."

The Vikings grabbed them and tied them up tight.

"They're going to destroy our time machine," said Harold as the Vikings prepared their bonfire. "We'll be stuck in the past forever!"

"Don't be silly," said Pigsticks. "We are Pigsticks and Harold! We're too important to spend our lives in an icy wasteland. There must be a way out."

Harold tried to cheer himself up.

"At least we still have my Battenburg cake," he said. "Would you like a piece?"

"Harold," said Pigsticks, "this is not the time for cake!"

Cake ... or Doom!

As night fell, the Vikings lit the bonfire.

"This is it," said Harold. "Our future's about to go up in flames."

"Nonsense!" said Pigsticks. "It's our past that's going up in flames. We have a very bright future."

But he didn't sound very certain.

Harold watched in silence as the Vikings carried the time machine toward the fire.

"There's something very familiar about these Vikings," said Pigsticks. "They're very strong for their size. Almost as strong as you, Harold. . . ."

"They're nothing like me," said Harold.

At that very moment, Hamfrida slipped on a dried fish. She tumbled to the ground, and her helmet fell off.

"She's a hamster!" cried Harold. "She *is* like me!"

"I thought as much!" said Pigsticks. "Everyone knows that hamsters take parties very seriously."

And then Harold had an amazing idea. "Pigsticks!" he cried. "Cake!"

"I already said no."

"No! I mean, hamsters love cake. And there wasn't any cake at the Vikings' party. I'd have smelled it."

"Maybe cake doesn't exist yet?" said Pigsticks.

"You mean these hamsters have never tasted cake before?" said Harold. "No wonder they're so angry — a hamster without cake is a grumpy hamster!"

"The Battenburg is our only hope," said Pigsticks.

Harold cleared his throat. "Excuse me, Hamfrida," he said. "This looks like a very lovely party — but I have something that will make it even better."

Hamfrida turned toward him slowly. "HOW DARE YOU!" she said. "NOTHING could make my party better! I throw the best parties in HISTORY!"

"We've seen quite a lot of history, and you definitely don't," said Harold. "A party isn't a party without Battenburg cake."

Hamfrida was suspicious.

"What's Battenburg cake?" she said.

"Set me free and I'll show you," said Harold.

Hamfrida stared at Harold for a moment — and then she cried, "UNTIE THE PRISONER!"

Harold held out the Battenburg. Hamfrida took a sniff, then a bite. Everyone held their breath.

"This cake is so pink, yet so yellow . . . so moist and delicious . . . so stupendous. . . . It's THE FOOD OF THE GODS!" said Hamfrida.

She made all the Vikings try the Battenburg. They agreed it was the best thing they'd ever eaten — even better than dried fish.

"How can we ever reward you for the gift of cake?" said Hamfrida.

"Could we have our silver throne back, please?" asked Harold. "We need it to get home."

"Oh, but that wouldn't be a gift!" said Hamfrida. "There must be something else."

"What we really need is something to replace the broken lever," said Harold. "Hamfrida . . . could we please have your ax?"

"My ax? You're welcome to it," said Hamfrida.

Hamfrida then had a terrific thought. "And in return," she said, "maybe you could give us the recipe for your wonderful cake?"

"I'd be delighted!" said Harold. "What an honor!"

Once Harold had taught the Vikings to make Battenburg, Hamfrida handed over her golden ax. Harold fit it into the time machine where the lever had been and set the time to the present day.

"But we need to go to the future," said Pigsticks. "I need to build a spaceship so I can win the Best Invention Prize at the science fair!"

Harold shook his head. "Absolutely not," he said. "Some things are more important than winning prizes. Like being alive, for instance."

And then Pigsticks said something Harold never thought he'd hear him say: "You're right."

Pigsticks and Harold climbed onto the time machine and each put a hand on the ax.

"Ready?" said Pigsticks. "One . . . two . . . three!"

Pigsticks and Harold crashed down in the middle of the science fair. Everyone in Tuptown was very surprised to see them.

"Where did you come from?" asked Milton.

"The past!" said Pigsticks.

"Nonsense," said Bobbins.

"It's true!" said Pigsticks. "We found this time machine in my attic and traveled through history!"

"Prove it!" said Bobbins.

"All right," said Pigsticks, standing up. "This, ladies and gentlepigs, is a genuine Viking ax."

"NO!" cried Harold.

"Don't touch it —"

But it was too late.

As soon as Pigsticks pulled the ax out, the time machine disappeared.

Harold was gone.

"Where is he?" asked Alice.

"He's lost in time," said Pigsticks. "He could be anywhere in history. And it's all my fault!"

"But what will we do without Harold?" cried Otterly. "Who'll make our birthday cakes for us?"

"Who'll water my garden when I'm on vacation?" said Alice with tears in her eyes.

FITZzz

"Who'll save the day when one of Pigsticks'
ridiculous ideas goes wrong?" asked Milton.

"He was my best friend," whimpered Pigsticks.
"Harold won't survive out there on his own."

Suddenly everything went dark. The room
began to shake. Light shone through a crack in
the door. . . .

"What's that?" whispered Pigsticks.

Everyone rushed outside — and there, on Tuptown Village Green, was a spaceship.

"Is it aliens?" asked Bonzo.

"Are we being invaded?" asked Sissy.

"Could it be — ?" said Pigsticks. But before he could finish, a tiny astronaut started walking slowly down the spaceship ramp.

The astronaut took off his helmet.

Everyone gasped.

It was Harold!

"You're back!" cried Pigsticks, overjoyed. "Where have you been?"

"Far into the future," said Harold. "And unlike the past, everyone was very friendly."

"That's a relief," said Pigsticks.

"I know," said Harold. "Anyway, some helpful moon hamsters showed me how to build a spaceship."

"And you did it all by yourself?" said Pigsticks.

"Yes, I suppose I did," said Harold proudly. "And this ship travels through time AND space!"

"You've been into space?" asked Milton.

"Of course I have," said Harold. "It's great, once you get used to endless silence and never-ending darkness. Do you want to see for yourself?"

"Do we ever!" cried Milton. "But before we go, I have an announcement. I hereby declare that the prize for best invention goes to: Harold!"

"Me?" said Harold. "I never win anything."

"Although . . . the spaceship was my idea, so I'm the winner really," said Pigsticks.

"I suppose you're right," said Harold.

"Let's go into space!" said Pirate George. "Power up the warp drive. It's time to . . ."

"What an adventure!" said Pigsticks. "I wonder where we'll end up next."

"I'd like to visit the Vikings again," said Harold. "I've got more cakes for them to try. Speaking of which, I brought this Atom Cake back from the future for you. Go on. Take a bite. . . ."